THE OGS DISCOVER FIRE

AND OTHER STUFF

● ●

A one-act play

by Alan Kramer
illustrated by Anita DuFalla

CAST OF CHARACTERS

● ●

Narrators   Amelia Earhart

The Ogs   Orville Wright

Christopher Columbus   Wilbur Wright

Henry Ford   Sally Ride

Charles Lindbergh

SETTING

● ●

The Ogs Discover Fire and Other Stuff takes place
"somewhere in time and space." It starts when the Ogs,
our ancestors, were living in caves, and moves up to
the present.

Some Suggestions on Casting, Staging, and Costumes

The play can be staged with many actors or with just a
few. For example, the narrators can be played by three
actors or by just one. The Ogs can be played by eight
different actors or by fewer actors having multiple roles.
The Ogs are dressed "Og-ishly" (for example, with
inside-out T-shirts).

Narrator A: *(stepping forward and speaking to the audience)* Hello, and welcome to *The Ogs Discover Fire and Other Stuff.*

Narrator B: Once upon a time—a really, really long time ago, even before the first video games—our earliest ancestors, the Ogs, appeared. *(The Ogs enter.)*

Narrator C: They weren't very developed yet. *(The Ogs look confused.)*

Narrator A: Let's face it, they had a long way to go. *(The Ogs look at one another and shrug.)*

Narrator B: For example, they didn't know how to use their thumbs.

Narrator A: Then one day while they were just hanging around, an Og named Bog suddenly looked down at his hand *(Bog looks at his hand)* and discovered his thumbs. *(Bog looks over at the Narrator, not sure what to do. Narrator wiggles her thumbs. Bog goes "ahhhh" and wiggles his thumbs.)* This was a very important discovery. *(Bog wiggles his thumbs at the other Ogs. He grunts, trying to get their attention.)*

Narrator C: Unfortunately, since they hadn't developed language yet, nobody had any idea what Bog was so excited about. *(Bog finally gets the others to notice his thumbs. They all make "ahhhh" sounds and hold their thumbs up.)*

Narrator A: With thumbs, they could do things they couldn't do before.

Narrator B: Like make signs to one another. *(The Ogs all make the "thumbs up" and "OK" signs to one another and the audience.)*

Narrator C: And, more important, they could pick things up. *(Cog picks up a flower with thumb and fingers and shows it around. The other Ogs gather around and look at it, not knowing what to do. Cog sniffs it. The other Ogs make "ahhhh" sounds and pick up things and sniff them, too.)*

Narrator A: But the big breakthrough came when the Ogs learned how to use tools. *(The Ogs try to use various things as tools— rocks, sticks, flowers, leaves, etc.)*

Narrator B: Of course, sometimes their thumbs got in the way. (*Fog swings a rock as a hammer and hits himself in the thumb.*)

Fog: Ow!

Other Ogs: (*imitating the sound*) Ow?

Fog: (*holding up his thumb*) Owwww!

Other Ogs: (*playing a game, holding up their thumbs and imitating Fog*) Oh. Owwww!

Fog: No! OWWWWW!!!!!

Gog: (*This stops the game.*) OK. What does *Ow* mean??

Fog: It means *it HURTS!!!!!!* (*Gog and Fog suddenly realize they've used words.*)

Narrator C: And so the Ogs developed language.

Jog: (*The other Ogs gather around Fog.*) You should have been more careful.

Mog: You should only use tools under supervision. Here, let me show you how to use that.

Tog: (*grabbing for it*) No. Me! I'll show him!

Narrator A: This led to the invention of arguing. (*The Ogs all start arguing and grabbing at things.*)

Narrator B: But this was just the beginning of invention among the— (*The arguing is so loud, the Narrator can't be heard.*) HEY!! (*The arguing stops.*)

Narrator C: And the Ogs thought to themselves (*the Ogs stop and put fingers to their heads, thinking*), "What other new things can we invent?" (*Zog steps forward. He's eating something and making a face. It doesn't taste very good.*)

Zog: Yuck. This tastes terrible.

Narrator A: Zog suddenly got an idea.

Zog: Hey! I've got an idea!

Bog: What??

Zog: Why don't we cook this stuff instead of eating it raw?

Cog: Yeah!! (*All the others call out in agreement.*)

Narrator B: The others all thought this was a terrific idea, too. Except for one problem.

Fog: Hey! *(The others stop.)* What does "cooking" mean?

Gog: I don't know, but I say we try it anyway. *(The Ogs all take food and do different things to it – banging it, twisting it, throwing it in the air or on the ground, etc.)*

Jog: Stop it! Cooking is when you heat things up, like on a fire, and…

Narrator C: They were about to make a very important breakthrough.

Mog: Whoa!! Time out! We haven't even discovered fire yet! *(The Ogs make "awwww" sounds. They start banging and rubbing things together—flowers, leaves, anything—trying to make fire. Nothing works.)*

Tog: *(holding up a flint and a rock)* How about this? *(Tog strikes them together. There's a "spark.")* Kindling! Quick! Get me some kindling!!

Other Ogs: What's kindling?

Tog: Little pieces of dry wood!

(The Ogs make "ahhhh" sounds and run off to get kindling. They pile it up. Tog strikes the rocks together. All start blowing on the kindling. Finally, they have… fire! [maybe a flashlight hidden among the sticks] They look at the "fire" a moment, then at one another. Suddenly, all but Tog and Zog run off, screaming in fear.)

Zog: Wait! Come back!! *(They're gone. Tog and Zog warm their hands by the fire.)* Ahhhh. *(One by one, the others return. Finally, Cog comes on, holding a marshmallow on a stick. Cog heats the marshmallow in the "fire" and eats it.)*

Cog: Mmmmm.

Bog: Good?

Cog: Mmmmmmmm!
(Other Ogs grab whatever they can find and "cook" it, saying "mmmmm" to everything, even rocks.)

Narrator B: The Ogs found that the fire kept them warm in the winter. *(They warm their hands by the fire.)*

Narrator C: And gave them light to see by. *(Some take out comic books to read.)*

Narrator A: It also kept wild animals away from their camps. *(They take out sticks to protect themselves against wild animals, but they don't need them now.)*

Narrator B: The Ogs were very happy. Their lives were just about perfect.

(All the Ogs are sitting comfortably near their fire. All except Jog, who's off on the side digging in the ground.)

Fog: What are you doing?

Jog: *(like a little kid who's been caught doing something bad)* Nothing.

Fog: Yes, you are. You're digging. What are you digging?

Jog: I'm planting seeds.

Gog: What for?

Jog: I'm going to grow crops—corn, wheat, tomatoes, apples, broccoli. In a little while, they'll come up, and we can eat them.

Mog: Up where?

Jog: Up out of the ground. *(The other Ogs laugh at this silly idea.)* It's true. You see these seeds? If I plant them in the ground, in just a few months, they'll turn into tomatoes. Or is it peaches? Anyhow, something will grow. Something we can eat.

Tog: In a few *months?* But we're Ogs. We can't wait around for a few months waiting for something to grow.

Zog: We move from place to place, and we eat whatever's growing there.

Jog: I don't want to do that anymore. I want to grow crops and live in one place for a change.

Mog: *(almost whining)* But we've always done it this way.

Jog: So? Who says we have to keep doing something just because *(imitating Mog)* we've always done it that way? *(The Ogs think about this. Jog keeps working.)*

Zog: But why do things have to change, Jog? Change is scary.

Jog: Don't you see? For the first time, we'll be able to choose where we want to live. We won't have to just wander around all the time looking for food.

Bog: You mean we could build houses, instead of just living in caves?

Jog: That's right!

Cog: What if we wanted to move somewhere warmer?

Jog: Then we could move there. We can plant our crops and build our houses anywhere we want.

Fog: *(catching on)* I want to live up in the mountains!

Jog: OK!

Gog: I want to live near the water!

Jog: Fine.

Mog: I want to live on the plains, where there's a lot of space.

Tog: I want to live in the city! *(Everyone stops.)*

Zog: What's a city?

Tog: It's a place where a lot of people live.
You can have big buildings and theaters and
museums and subways and football teams
and movies.

Bog: I want to live far away, across the oceans!
(Everyone stops.)

Cog: You can't do that! The world is a big flat
disk that rides on the back of a turtle.
Everybody knows that! You'll fall off the ends
of it if you go too far. *(Narrator C steps forward
and rings a bell [or something]. Christopher
Columbus enters, dressed in the kind of costume
you'd expect in 1492.)*

Columbus: *(entering)* No you won't.

Fog: Who are you?

Columbus: I'm Christopher Columbus. And I'm
here to tell you that the world is not a flat disk.
It is round.

Gog: Round? How do you know that?

Columbus: Because I've sailed around it. I left Spain in 1492, planning to sail west to India. But instead I discovered America.

Jog: Spain? India? America? I've never heard of any of these places.

Columbus: That's because none of this has happened yet.

Mog: I don't get it.

Bog: So we won't fall off the ends of the earth?

Columbus: No. I promise.

Cog: Will we meet different people in these other countries?

Columbus: Yes, you will. The world is filled with different peoples.

Fog: Do they speak different languages?

Columbus: Yes, hundreds of different languages.

Gog: Wow! How are we going to communicate with all these people?

Jog: We don't know any other languages!

Columbus: You could start with something simple, like pictures. *(The Ogs think about this a moment. Cog has an idea. She slowly walks over to the fire and takes out the burnt stick from the marshmallow. She walks over to the wall and starts drawing.)*

Narrator A: And that's how the first writing began—with drawings on a wall. Breakthroughs come in all kinds of ways and when you least expect them.

Tog: *(looking over Cog's shoulder as she draws)* Hey. That's a mastodon, right?

Zog: This one looks like a saber-tooth tiger.

Bog: And that's a woolly mammoth! You're really good at this!

Gog: But I can't draw very well. I wish we didn't have to use pictures to communicate!

Mog: Words! Let's write down words! *(The Ogs love the idea, but…)*

Tog: *(upset)* I don't know how to write!!

Narrator C: After some discussion *(The Ogs discuss it a minute)*, they decided they could put the words together using…

Zog: Letters! Let's make words out of letters!

Tog: *(excited now)* Letters! Let's use letters! What are letters?!

Zog: Let's just try making some and see what happens. *(They all start scratching away at making letters.)*

Bog: *(finally)* I've got one!! *(He holds up a rock with the letter A scratched in it.)*

Cog: What is that?

Bog: The letter A! This is the first official letter!

Fog: *(holding up the letter B made from twigs [or something])* Here's B!

Gog: C!

Fog: Of course I see. I'm sitting right next to you!

Gog: I meant the letter C!

Fog: Oh. Why didn't you say that?

Zog: I've invented W!

Mog: You have not! That's an M—M for Mog! (*They pull and push at one another. Finally, Mog turns Zog's letter M-side-up.*)

Zog: (*pulling it away and turning it W-side-up*) W!!!!!

Tog: (*holding up a T*) This is a T! T for Tog!

Cog: C for Cog!

Fog: How many is that?

Gog: I don't know. We haven't invented numbers yet.

Bog: I want to buy a vowel!

Cog: What do you think this is, *Wheel of Fortune?*

Narrator A: All of a sudden, out of the blue, another breakthrough!

The Ogs: The wheel! Let's invent the wheel!! (*Some of the Ogs start running around, excited, yelling "The wheel! The wheel!"*)

Fog: Hold it!! (*yelling, making them stop*) What's a wheel?

Jog: (*realizing*) I don't know.

Narrator B: Breakthroughs don't always come that fast.

Gog: Hey! I thought we were inventing writing!

Tog: No! The wheel! The wheel!

Gog: Writing's more important than some silly wheel!

Tog: More important than the wheel?? You must be kidding! (*Everyone starts taking sides, yelling "writing!" or "the wheel!" as loud as they can.*)

Columbus: Hold it!! HOLD IT!! (*Everyone finally stops.*) Why don't you guys work on writing, and you guys can invent the wheel?

Zog: Now that's a good idea. (*Some of the Ogs go back to their letters. The others just stand there, not knowing where to start.*)

Narrator C: What's the problem?

Fog: *(raising a hand)* We still don't know what a wheel is.

Columbus: *(trying to help out, making rolling motions)* Think…rolling. Something that rolls. *(They look at him, still confused.)* It goes around and around. *(They still don't understand.)*

Gog: *(one of the letter carvers, holding up a rock)* I have an O!

Jog: Shh! We're inventing the wheel over here!

Tog: But look! *(taking it from Gog and holding it up)* This is a wheel!

Jog: Gog said that was an O.

Tog: It's an O and a wheel. Look! *(Tog rolls it noisily along the ground.)*

Bog: Somebody had better hurry up and invent tires.

Cog: *(looking at the wheel just sitting there)* I don't know. It's not right yet.

Zog: We're missing something.

Cog: (*picking up the wheel*) I've got an idea. (*Cog heads off with the wheel. Zog runs off after Cog. As they do, Mog steps forward.*)

Mog: I've got it!

Other Ogs: What?

Mog: How the letters all fit together! (*Mog gathers the Narrators and Columbus together and whispers to them a moment.*)

Mog, Columbus, and Three Narrators:
(*singing the familiar nursery rhyme:*)

A, B, C, D, E, F, G,
H, I, J, K, L-M-N-O-P,
Q-R-S, T-U-V,
W, X, Y, and Z.
Now that we know our ABCs, we can
write whatever we please!
(*They bow to the audience.*)

Cog: (*Cog and Zog come back on, pulling a child's wagon. Everyone stares at them.*) What? What? See? This is what you do with wheels.

Zog: We made a wagon!!

Bog: *(getting the idea)* I get it! Wheels roll. *(Cog nods "yes.")* So if you attach them to something—

Fog: …you can pull things around—heavy things, like rocks.

Gog: Or people. *(pointing at all the Ogs)* Now if we want to go someplace, we can get in our wagon and ride! *(All the Ogs try to pile into the wagon. They can't fit. Finally, Jog and Bog get in. Zog tries to pull them.)*

Zog: There's got to be an easier way to do this.

Jog: Maybe if we had something to pull it.

Tog: If there were only a way of combining fire and wheels.

Fog: Using fire with the wheels??

Tog: Right! If we could use the fire to turn the wheels—(*All the Ogs think hard about this a moment. All of a sudden, another bell rings, and Henry Ford comes on. [He's in a costume to look like Henry Ford.]*)

Ford: I might be able to help you with that.

Cog: Who…? Who are you?

Ford: I'm Henry Ford. (*The Ogs and Columbus look at him blankly*)

Columbus: Is that supposed to mean something to us? We're just up to the wheel.

Ford: I invented the Model T. (*The Ogs and Columbus shrug.*) The first mass-produced car? (*They still don't understand.*) Brrrum! Brrrum!!

The Ogs: Ahhh! (*Now they've got it!*) Brrrum! Brrrum!! (*They all pretend they're driving around, making Brrrum! Brrrum!! sounds.*)

BRRUMM BRRUM

Ford: Exactly. Now you can take your wagon and add a motor.

Tog: What's a motor?

Ford: *(explaining slowly so they can follow)* You make a box out of metal. Then you put fire into it. And it makes the wheels go around. Brrrum! Brrrum!!

Cog: I get it! The energy from the fire turns the wheels!

Ford: That's right. Of course, you also have to have gas and spark plugs and a carburetor. And then you'll need gas stations and parking lots and toll booths on the highway and… *(He suddenly notices that everyone is staring at him.)* But we'll get to that later.

Zog: *(looking up at the sky)* It sounds too complicated. Why don't we just grow wings? Then we could fly like the birds.

Charles Lindbergh: *(entering with Amelia Earhart, to another bell)* We can help you there.

Bog: Who are you?

Lindbergh: I'm Charles Lindbergh.

Earhart: And I'm Amelia Earhart. We're the most famous pilots of our age.

Cog: What are pilots?

Lindbergh: We fly airplanes.

Fog: (*looking at Ford*) Airplanes?

Ford: They're like my cars, only with wings.

Gog: And you guys flew them in the sky? Like birds?

Lindbergh: That's right. I was the first man to fly alone across the Atlantic Ocean.

Earhart: And I was the first woman to fly across the Pacific Ocean.

Jog: So you two invented flying?

Lindbergh: (*laughing*) No, no, no!

Earhart: Most inventions are the work of many people. (*She calls out.*) Orville! Wilbur! (*Another bell rings. The Wright brothers come on.*) The Wright brothers.

Orville: We designed the first plane ever to fly under its own power.

Wilbur: But we based our designs on work other people had done.

Orville: All of it going back to you.

Mog: Us? *(The Wright brothers nod.)* We started all that?

Sally Ride: *(entering to another bell)* I got to be the first American woman in space because Zog had the idea of flying like the birds. I bet you never thought we'd be flying around in space. *(Zog shakes his head "no.")*

Ford: *(noticing that Fog is off sitting alone, looking sad.)* What's the matter?

Fog: It sounds like all the important break-throughs have already been made. What's left for anyone else to do?

Columbus: Are you kidding! There are always new things to discover.

Lindbergh: Someone will always be working to develop a faster plane.

Earhart: And a safer one. My plane crashed while I was flying around the world.

Sally Ride: We still need someone to cure the common cold.

Orville: And someday someone is going to invent ice cream that doesn't melt!

Ford: Hey! We'd better get to work. We've got a lot to do!

Columbus: You're right. (*to the Ogs*) Thanks again—for everything! (*Ford, Columbus, and the rest head off together, leaving the Ogs alone.*)

Jog: (*after a second, calling after them*) Hey! Wait! You guys want some help?

Sally Ride: (*from offstage*) Sure. Come on! (*The Ogs all run off together.*)

Bog: (*running back on for a second*) The end!

Fog: (*running back on*) No! To be continued! (*They run back off.*)

THE END